CONTENTS

NODDY

ANNUAL 2005

Published by Pedigree Books Limited
Beech Hill House, Walnut Gardens, Exeter, Devon EX4 4DH.
E-mail books@pedigreegroup.co.uk
Published 2004

WELCOME TO TOYLAND

Hello, everyone!
My name is Noddy and this is my little aeroplane. Mr. Sparks has just mended it for me, so I'm giving it a clean before I fly it again. Do you want to know why my aeroplane needed mending? Well, you can read all about that later in the annual. Needless to say it had something to do with those naughty goblins! There are lots of other Toyland adventures for you to read about, as well as puzzles, rhymes and games. Before I give the aeroplane a last polish, let me take you to meet my friends from Toy Town...

NODDY'S CAR

I don't often travel by aeroplane. Usually, I drive round in my little red and yellow car. It is the Toy Town taxi and I'm always busy taking passengers around Toyland. Everyone knows the "Parp! Parp!" of my car horn.

BIG-EARS

Big-Ears is my best friend. He always makes delicious teas for me at his house in Toadstool Wood. You will soon see how I once made a little mistake when I fetched some eggs for him and he was rather cross!

TESSIE BEAR AND BUMPY DOG

Tessie Bear is another good friend. She has a bouncy pet called Bumpy Dog, who is often so pleased to see me that he knocks me over! Tessie Bear also keeps chickens, so I always know where to go for fresh eggs.

MR. SPARKS

Mr. Sparks is very clever. Not only can he mend anything with an engine, he invents things, too. He runs the Toy Town garage and makes sure that all our cars have the petrol and oil that they need.

MISS PINK CAT

The best ice-cream in town is made by Miss Pink Cat. She also makes marvellous milk shakes! Miss Pink Cat has only ever lived in a town, so she knows little about the countryside, as you will soon find out.

MR. PLOD

Toy Town's policeman is Mr. Plod. If he thinks someone is breaking the law, he will blow his whistle and shout, "Stop, in the name of Plod!" He likes a good case to solve, but we all know that the goblins are usually to blame!

MASTER TUBBY BEAR

Master Tubby Bear lives near me and often comes knocking at my door if he wants to play a game of football. We have the best fun when it snows and we build snowmen together.

DINAH DOLL

Toy Town market's best stall is run by Dinah Doll. When she's not selling things, Dinah is busy organising special days to make the market more interesting. You will have fun reading about what happened on Chocolate Day!

SLY AND GOBBO

Sly and Gobbo are the naughty goblins from the Dark Wood. The troublesome twosome are always up to mischief and play the silliest tricks on me. At least Mr. Plod makes sure they always get caught!

A BOY CALLED...

His first is in jingle (the noise his hat makes),
His second's in chocolate - on his favourite cakes!
His third's in the kindness he shows to his friends,
His fourth's in the gardens he carefully tends,
His fifth's in a boy who will help anybody,
His whole is what name? You've guessed it, it's Noddy!

NODDY BY NUMBERS

Here is Noddy outside his House-For-One. Hello, Noddy! Use your crayons or pens to colour the picture by numbers, using these colours:
1. red 2. dark blue 3. light blue 4. yellow 5. pink 6. brown 7. green

GOBLINS ABOVE!

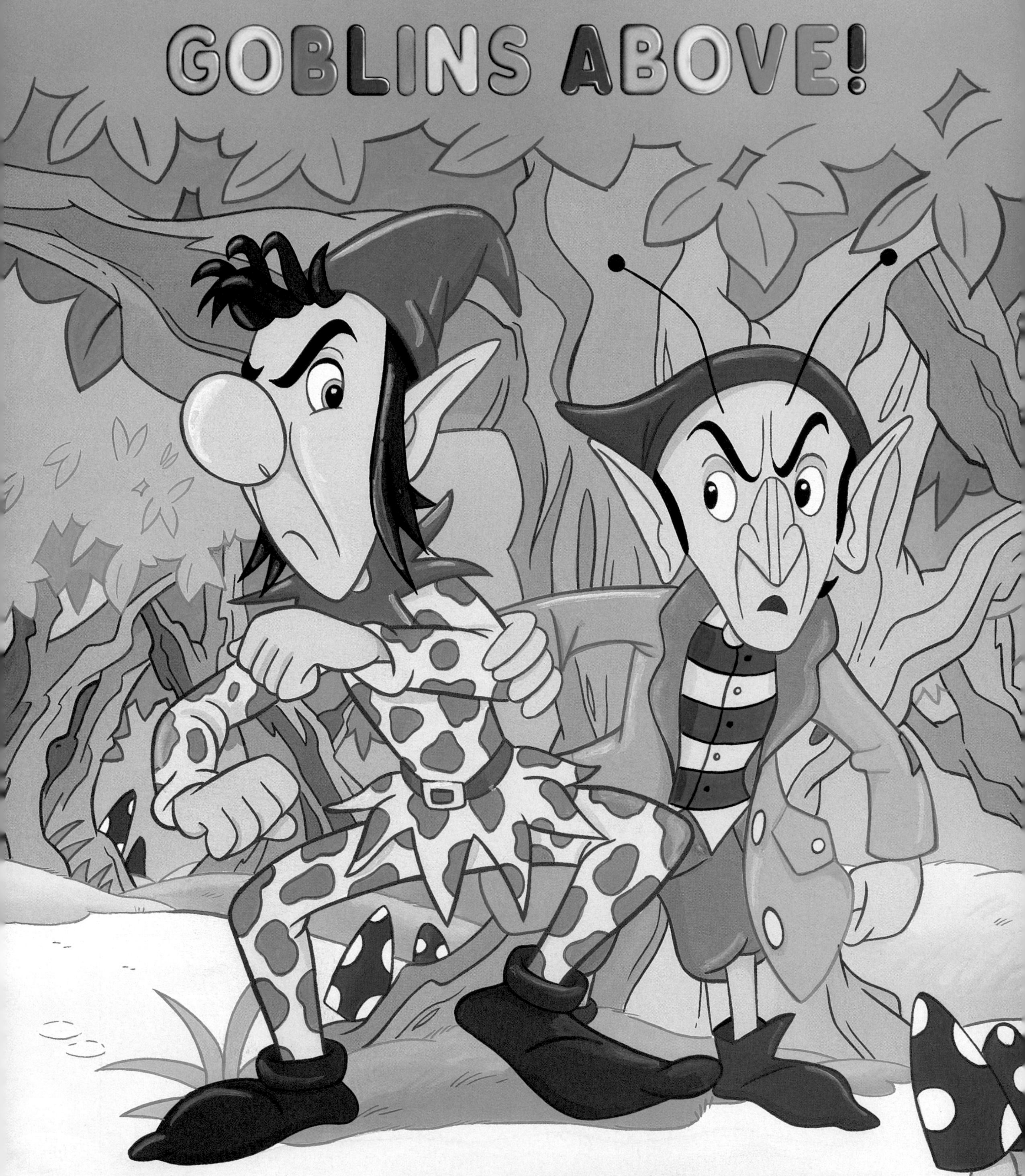

Deep in the Dark Wood, Sly and Gobbo were looking out for Noddy's car. "Do you see anything yet?" asked Sly. "Yes, an ugly sight!" snapped Gobbo, getting ready to push Sly aside. "You! Move out of the way!"

Gobbo frowned. "Where's he got to with our parcel?" he wondered aloud. "We can't very well steal his car if he's not here." A sudden noise from above startled the goblins. "It's Noddy!" they exclaimed. "He's in his aeroplane!"

"Good morning, goblins!" Noddy called down to Sly and Gobbo. "Here's your parcel! Sorry about the noisy aeroplane - Mr. Sparks is just mending my little taxi. Must fly!" The two goblins gazed after Noddy as he sped away.

"How are we going to steal Noddy's car now, Gobbo?" asked Sly. "Never mind his car," sneered Gobbo, "we'll have his plane instead!"

Big-Ears came out of his Toadstool House to see what the noise was. "Ah, an airmail parcel!" he chuckled, picking up Noddy's delivery.

When Noddy had delivered his parcels, he landed the aeroplane. Mr. Sparks had almost finished mending the red and yellow car. "Thank you very much, Mr. Sparks," said Noddy. "It's no trouble," smiled Mr. Sparks.

That afternoon, Sly and Gobbo went to where Noddy kept his aeroplane. "Here it is," said Gobbo, climbing in. Sly was not so sure. "We don't know how to fly a plane, Gobbo," he pointed out. "It could go out of control."

"Are you getting in or not?" Gobbo sighed, starting up the engine. Sly took a deep breath and scrambled into the passenger seat. "We have lift off!" cackled Gobbo, suddenly sending the aeroplane upwards.

Noddy had finished delivering all his parcels and was out for a walk with Bumpy Dog. "Fetch, boy!" he called, throwing a stick for him.

The goblins swooped down from nowhere in the aeroplane and Sly grabbed the stick. "Hey!" shouted Noddy. "That's Bumpy Dog's stick!"

"Hey!" Noddy gasped. "That's MY aeroplane!" "It's ours now!" sang Sly as they zoomed off again. "Come back at once!" Noddy shouted angrily, chasing the aeroplane with Bumpy at his heels. "Bring back my plane!"

Dinah Doll was selling googleberry muffins from her stall. "They look delicious!" remarked Mr. Plod. Suddenly, the goblins sped down over the market with a WHOOSH! "Stop in the name of Plod!" shouted the angry policeman.

Sly and Gobbo flew on towards Toadstool Wood. "There's Big-Ears!" exclaimed Sly, pointing down below. "Then let's say hello," grinned Gobbo, sending the plane down so low that poor Big-Ears had to run inside to safety.

Noddy hurried to see if his friend was all right. "Big-Ears, the goblins took my plane!" he explained. "I can see that," said Big-Ears.

Noddy did not know what to do. "We should do nothing," Big-Ears said, wisely. "They can't stay up there forever, you see."

As always, Big-Ears was right. There was very little petrol left in the aeroplane, so its engine soon stopped running. "W-what's happening?" asked Sly, as they began to fall from the sky. "I don't know!" snapped Gobbo.

As the plane hurtled towards a farm below, Gobbo steered it into a haystack. THWUMP! They landed. "There they are!" shouted Noddy. Mr. Plod blew his whistle and Big-Ears joined the race to the haystack.

The goblins' knees were still shaking as they got out of the aeroplane. "Sly and Gobbo, come with me to the station!" boomed Mr. Plod, taking them away. "Cheer up, you two," Noddy chuckled. "At least you had a soft landing!"

MR. SPARKS' SPARE PARTS

Mr. Sparks mends all the things with wheels in Toy Town. He will have to mend Noddy's aeroplane, now that the naughty goblins have broken it! Use a pencil to help Mr. Sparks with his repairs by matching the vehicles to their parts.

MAIL MISCHIEF

Those naughty goblins have rubbed some of the letters from the names on these parcels. Now Noddy doesn't know where to deliver them! Help Noddy by filling in the letters and telling him which Toy Town person each parcel is for. The answers are at the bottom of the page.

2. Mr. W_bb_y M_n

1. Mi_ _ Pi_k C_t

3. Mas_e_ T_bb_ Be_r

4. Di_ah D_l_

5. Ma_th_ Mo_ke_

Answers: 1. Miss Pink Cat 2. Mr. Wobbly Man 3. Master Tubby Bear 4. Dinah Doll 5. Martha Monkey

CAR WASH

Sly and Gobbo spend their days
Taking people's things,
Things with engines, things with wheels,
Even things with wings!

Gobbo once stole Big-Ears' bike
And Sly pinched Noddy's car,
They went too fast, there was a CRASH!
This time they'd gone too far.

"You naughty goblins, come with me,"
Said Mr. Plod with a frown,
"You won't go home till you have cleaned
Every car and bike in town!"

FLYING SLY

Sly thought it would be fun to be towed along by Noddy's car on his roller-skates. Noddy did not know he had an extra passenger, though, and drove quickly round a bend. Sly lost control and it serves him right!

Look at the two pictures and see if you can spot the five differences between them. When you have found them all, use your pens or crayons to colour the picture below, copying the colours from the opposite page.

Answers: 1. Different bug 2. Extra flower 3. Different chimney 4. Cloud in the sky 5. Open boot on Noddys car

Noddy was busy washing his car one morning, when his best friend Big-Ears cycled up. "Good morning, Big-Ears!" Noddy called. "Good morning, Noddy," Big-Ears replied. "I hope you're not too busy to run an errand for me."

Noddy was always happy to help, so he said he would gladly do something for Big-Ears. "Mr. Plod is coming round for tea this afternoon," Big-Ears explained, "and I would like you to fetch me some of Tessie Bear's fresh eggs."

Noddy said goodbye to Big-Ears and rinsed his car. "I should go straight to Tessie Bear's now," he thought to himself, "otherwise I might forget those eggs." Off went Noddy in his car, with a 'Parp! Parp!' on his car horn.

Noddy went into the kitchen, where Tessie Bear was busy making some of her delicious cakes. "Hello, Noddy," she smiled. "What brings you here?"

"Hello, Tessie Bear," said Noddy. "I'd like some eggs for Big-Ears, please." Tessie Bear said she had already collected the eggs that morning.

"I sent most of the eggs to the market earlier," she explained, "but you should still be able to find some if you look hard enough." Tessie Bear gave Noddy a basket for his eggs and showed him to the hen houses.

Noddy looked in the hen houses, but he could not find a single egg. "Hello, hen," he said to one the hens. "Can you show me where the eggs are, please?" "Cluck! Cluck!" replied the startled hen, scuttling away.

Noddy came to a plump mother hen sitting on its nest. "Hello, hen," he whispered this time. "Do you have any eggs under there?"

"Cluck! Cluck!" replied the hen, proudly standing up to show off her nest full of eggs. "Oh, yes, you have lots!" said Noddy.

Noddy carefully put the eggs into his basket, one by one. "Just what I need," he smiled, not seeing that the poor hen was upset.

"Cluck! Cluck!" shrieked the hen, pecking Noddy's hand. "Ouch!'" gasped Noddy, backing away. "That's not very nice, hen!"

Noddy hurried away from the hen houses, but the angry hen chased him all the way back to his car. "Come on, little car," Noddy said, starting up the engine and setting off. "I don't know why Mrs. Hen is so cross with me."

Noddy drove straight to Big-Ears' Toadstool House to deliver the eggs. "Hello!" he called as he went in, but Big-Ears was still out. His cat was there alone, dozing in front of the fire. "Hello, Whiskers," Noddy smiled.

Noddy put the basket of eggs on the table. "I shall leave them here," he said, "so that Big-Ears sees them when he comes in."

Later, Whiskers thought she heard a noise. She padded over to the table and tried to peep into the basket. There it was again!

When Big-Ears finally returned home, he stood and stared in amazement. There were fluffy, yellow chicks hopping about his living room! "Oh, my! Whiskers!" he exclaimed. "Where on earth have all these chicks come from?"

Big-Ears' cat was chasing the chicks, so he picked her up. "No, Whiskers," he scolded gently. "You mustn't chase the poor little things."

Just as Big-Ears was wondering if Noddy had played a trick on him, Noddy arrived. "Big-Ears!" he smiled. "Did you get your lovely eggs - oh!"

Noddy was as surprised to see the chicks as Big-Ears had been. "What are they doing here?" he asked innocently. "You should know, Noddy," Big-Ears replied. "Show me the 'lovely', newly-laid eggs you brought."

Noddy was astonished to see only eggshells in the basket. They weren't newly-laid eggs at all! Big-Ears told him to return the chicks and say sorry to Tessie Bear - and to the hen. Back to the hen houses you go, Noddy!

BUMPY BEGS

Noddy's brought some eggs home
And now it's time for tea,
Scrambled, poached, or maybe fried,
Which is it to be?

What about an omelette?
Perhaps toad-in-the-hole?
Boiled egg with soldiers might be nice,
So would an egg roll.

Bumpy Dog is hungry, too,
He jumps up and he begs,
Oh, Bumpy Dog! What have you done?
You've broken all the eggs!

HOW MANY EGGS?

Noddy has come back to Tessie Bear's house to get a dozen eggs for Big-Ears. He is not quite sure, though, exactly how many a dozen eggs is! Help Noddy to count the eggs and find out how many make a dozen by filling in the missing numbers.

EASTER EGG HUNT

Noddy likes hen's eggs, but he loves chocolate eggs! At Easter, Big-Ears always does a chocolate egg hunt in Toadstool Wood for his Toy Town friends. Help Noddy, Martha Monkey and Clockwork Mouse to find four eggs each, then use your crayons or pencils to colour the picture.

MISS PINK CAT'S COUNTRY ADVENTURE

It was a warm summer day in Toy Town. Miss Pink Cat's Ice-cream Parlour had not even opened and there was a queue outside the door. "I'm looking forward to a nice, cool milkshake," said Mr. Wobbly Man. "I want an ice-cream!" said Master Tubby Bear.

The queue got longer, but still Miss Pink Cat did not open the door. Martha Monkey knocked impatiently. "Come on, Miss Pink Cat!" she called. "It's time your ice-cream parlour was open!" The others murmured in agreement.

The door opened a little and Miss Pink Cat peeped out. "I'm very sorry, everyone," she said anxiously, "but I can't open just yet. The milk has not arrived, you see. Wait there, and I will be back very soon."

Miss Pink Cat left her disappointed customers and rushed to the market. "Can I have some milk, please?" she asked Dinah Doll.

Dinah Doll explained that there had not been a milk delivery. "You could try going to where the milk comes from," she said.

Miss Pink Cat thanked Dinah Doll for her help, but then did not know what to do next. "Where does the milk come from?" she wondered. Then she heard a 'Parp! Parp!' and put out her arm. "Noddy! Stop!" she called.

Noddy stopped for Miss Pink Cat. "Where would you like to go, Miss Pink Cat?" he asked. Miss Pink Cat was not sure. "I'd like to go to...where the milk comes from," she said, hoping Noddy knew where that was.

"It's where the eggs come from, too!" Noddy smiled. Miss Pink Cat was puzzled. She thought that both milk and eggs came from the shop. She was surprised when they arrived at a country farm and Noddy said, "Here we are."

The farmer came out and told his visitors that he was still mending the milking machines, so there was no milk yet. Miss Pink Cat was upset.

"You're welcome to get some milk the old-fashioned way," said the farmer, giving Miss Pink Cat a bucket. "Oh!" she gasped, surprised.

"I think Miss Pink Cat means thank you," smiled Noddy. Off they both went to find the cows. Miss Pink Cat looked at some pigs and wondered if they would give her milk. "Here are the cows," said Noddy.

Miss Pink Cat held out her bucket towards one of the animals Noddy was pointing at. When nothing happened, she said politely, "I'd like some milk, please, cow." Noddy realised that his friend really was a town cat.

"Oh, please don't laugh at me!" exclaimed Miss Pink Cat. "I admit it, I know nothing about cows or milk or farms or - or -"

"It's all right, Miss Pink Cat," Noddy said gently. "Don't get upset. Why didn't you ask for help earlier? I'll tell you all you need to know."

Noddy explained that the milk was in the cow. "The cow drank all the milk?" gasped Miss Pink Cat. "Um, not quite," chuckled Noddy.

The farmer agreed to let Noddy and Miss Pink Cat take a cow with them, as they needed milk so urgently. They set off back to Toy Town.

Noddy said he would milk the cow while Miss Pink Cat served the customers. "Look, everyone!" he said to the waiting queue. "Miss Pink Cat has brought a cow here so you can have extra fresh milk!" The customers were delighted.

Miss Pink Cat soon opened the doors and her ice-cream parlour was serving again. Noddy was very good at milking the cow and poured the milk into the ice-cream machine so that the customers could have delicious, fresh ice-cream .

Miss Pink Cat thanked Noddy for all his help and for teaching her about cows. "You still have one lesson to learn," Noddy smiled, taking her to the door, "and that is to always shut the farm gate behind you!"

MARVELLOUS MILK

Now Miss Pink Cat knows where milk comes from, she needs to learn that all sorts of food can be made from it! Colour in all the things you think are made from milk and say whether you like them. Which of the foods shown here are not made from milk?

I LOVE MILK!

Milk on my cornflakes,
Milk in my tea,
If all the cows stopped giving milk,
Where would we be?

There'd be no cheese or yogurt,
Or butter for my toast,
There'd be no shakes or ice-cream -
They're what I like the most!

Trifle without custard,
Fruit pie with no cream,
Macaroni without sauce,
How dull those things would seem!

AMAZING ANIMALS

Miss Pink Cat has learnt which animal milk comes from, but she's not sure which animals give us these other things! Help Miss Pink Cat by drawing a line from each picture to the animal you think it comes from.

WHO SAID THAT?

Miss Pink Cat now knows that cows say "moo". Do you remember what the angry hen said to Noddy when he took her eggs? Use your pencil to practise writing these animal noises and make the noise when you finish each one!

WHAT SHOULD I READ?

So many stories, what should I read?
Something exciting, that's what I need,
The one about the beanstalk? The one with the three bears?
What about the ark one, with its animals in pairs?

Jungle stories, fairy tales, fables and rhymes,
Stories in the future, tales from olden times,
Animals and giants, people who take flight,
Oh, so many stories - I wish I had all night!

NODDY'S BEDTIME STORIES

Chocolate Day In Toy Town
Noddy And The Rainbow
Noddy's Lucky Day

CHOCOLATE DAY IN TOY TOWN

It was a special day in Toy Town market and Dinah Doll was busy preparing for it.
"Are you excited about our Chocolate Day, Master Tubby Bear?" she asked, as she decorated her stall.
"It's my favourite day," replied Master Tubby Bear. "I love it even more than Lollipop Day!"
Dinah Doll had organised the Chocolate Day and wanted to give a chocolate to every person in Toy Town. She looked at her watch.
"Noddy should be here soon," she said. "He's collecting the chocolate delivery from the station."

With a 'Parp! Parp!' of his car horn, Noddy drew up and brought one of two large boxes over to the stall. "Here's the first box of chocolates," he said, putting it down. "Be careful not to leave them in the sun, or they will melt."
Master Tubby Bear licked his lips.
"That would be fun," he smiled. "I could slurp up all the yummy chocolate puddles!"
Noddy and Dinah Doll laughed.
"I could eat a whole mountain of chocolate," he told them.
"Then you would turn into a chocolate bear," chuckled Noddy.
"And too much chocolate gives you a tummy ache," Dinah Doll warned. Master Tubby Bear insisted that he could eat all the chocolate in Toyland and more.

When Tessie Bear arrived in a new pink hat, Noddy and Dinah Doll were so busy saying how nice she looked that they did not notice Master Tubby Bear going over to Noddy's car. He was very excited about Chocolate Day and could wait no longer. Checking that no one was watching, he snatched up the box and hurried away with it. He sat in a quiet place nearby, then opened the box and grinned. He had never seen so many chocolates. He took one and ate it quickly. It was delicious. He took another, then another, then a handful, pushing them into his already full mouth.

It wasn't long before they were all gone and his tummy felt very full indeed. "Perhaps I'll just rest here a while," he groaned, feeling a little sick. He was so full of chocolate that he soon fell asleep and began dreaming. In his dream, he picked up a coin from the floor...and it turned to chocolate! He thought this was wonderful until he went to stroke Bumpy Dog and he turned to chocolate, too.

Before he knew what was happening, he had scratched his head and turned himself into chocolate!
"Mmm, look!" he heard Noddy say. "A delicious chocolate teddy bear!"
"Ooh, yes," agreed Dinah Doll. "We can eat him instead of the missing chocolates."
"Can I have a piece?" asked Tessie Bear.

"No! No!" Master Tubby Bear cried, waking himself up. He was astonished to see Noddy and Mr. Plod peering at him.

"Are you all right, Master Tubby Bear?" asked Noddy, gently.

"Do you have something to tell us, Master Tubby Bear?" asked Mr. Plod, not so gently.

"I think we've solved the case of the missing chocolates, Noddy," he added, tapping the empty box.

"I think you need to come and say sorry to Dinah Doll," said Noddy, helping Master Tubby Bear to his feet.

Dinah Doll gave a little smile when she heard that Master Tubby Bear had eaten enough chocolates to give him nightmares.

"I'm sorry for being so greedy," he said, holding his tummy. "I've ruined your Chocolate Day and I feel rather sick."

"I think you've learnt your lesson," said Dinah Doll. "Luckily for you, I ordered more than enough, so we can still enjoy Chocolate Day."

Dinah Doll opened the other box of chocolates and began to give them out to the delighted crowd.

"Would you like to join in the chocolate games later?" she asked.

"No, thank you," groaned Master Tubby Bear. "I'm going home for a lie down...and I shan't be eating chocolate again for a long, long time!"

NODDY AND THE RAINBOW

Tessie Bear loves flowers. One morning, she asked Noddy to drive her to the station so that she could take a train to the countryside.
"I'm taking some paper and crayons," she told him on the way, "to draw all the wild flowers that I find."
"I'd love to see those pictures when I pick you up," smiled Noddy, stopping at Toy Town station. "I hope it doesn't rain, though. Look at that cloud!"
Tessie Bear looked up and saw a strange, grey cloud looming overhead. "I've brought my umbrella, just in case," she said, getting out of the car. "Thank you, Noddy. See you at three o'clock!"

Later that day, something very strange happened. It did rain in Toy Town. Not only that, the big raindrops did something that they had never done before: they washed away all the colours!
"What's happened to my car?" Noddy gasped, when the rain had stopped. He looked down. "My clothes! They've lost all their colour, too!"

There was a terrible commotion as everyone realised what had happened.
"All we have left is black, white and grey!" cried Dinah Doll, holding up some balloons. "Who will want to buy grey balloons?"
"And who is going to eat grey googleberry ice-cream? Nobody!" added Miss Pink Cat. "You can say that again, Miss Pink Cat," said Big-Ears, "or should I call you Miss Grey Cat?" Miss Pink Cat shrieked in alarm as she looked down at her grey fur.

When it was time for Noddy to collect Tessie Bear, she was astonished to see that Toy Town's colours had vanished.
"I'm glad the funny cloud didn't rain on you," Noddy told her. "At least you still have your colours."
Tessie Bear wondered if they could use her crayons to colour everything in again. It seemed like a good idea at first, as she and Noddy set about colouring in the flowers and the lamp-posts. Their arms soon got tired, though, and they realised the crayons would run out before the town was finished.

"What are we going to do, Noddy?" asked Tessie Bear. "We can't let Toy Town stay like this."
"Look over there," Noddy smiled suddenly. Tessie Bear turned to see what had cheered Noddy up. "A rainbow!" she gasped. "Aren't its colours beautiful?"
Noddy thought the rainbow should share its colours with them to make Toy Town normal again. He asked Tessie Bear to get in the car and they drove to get his aeroplane.

Noddy borrowed a bucket from Mr. Sparks on the way and they went up in the aeroplane with it. First, Noddy tried to get his own colours back.
"Hold on tight!" he told Tessie Bear. WHOOSH! He raced the aeroplane right through the top of the rainbow.
"Noddy, it worked!" exclaimed Tessie Bear. "Your colours are back!"

Noddy told Tessie Bear to hold out the bucket while he sped through the rainbow a second time. She then held on to it tightly until Noddy flew down low over Toy Town and she could tip all the colours out.
"Look!" cried Mr. Wobbly Man down below. "Our colours are back!"
Dinah Doll waved her colourful balloons and cried, "Thank you, Noddy! Thank you, Tessie Bear!" Everyone cheered and thought that Toy Town looked even better and brighter than it did before.

When Noddy and Tessie Bear returned, they got a very warm welcome.
"On behalf of the whole town, I would like to thank you both for giving us back our colours," announced Mr. Plod, to loud applause.
"I couldn't have put up with all that grey for much longer," chuckled Noddy.
"Oh, Mr. Jumbo!" gasped Tessie Bear. "I'm so sorry, I must have missed you! Perhaps I can colour you in with a crayon?"
Everybody laughed. Do you know why? Mr. Jumbo is an elephant, and you know what colour they are supposed to be!

NODDY'S LUCKY DAY

Mr. Sparks was trying out his latest invention when he heard the 'Parp! Parp!' of Noddy's car.

"Hello, Noddy," he smiled. "Have you come for your special car oil?"

"Yes, Mr. Sparks," Noddy replied. "Ooh, that looks interesting," he added, looking at the machine. "What is it?"

Mr. Sparks explained that it was a fortune-telling machine. All Noddy had to do was put in a coin, push the button and wait for a card to drop out.

"Tomorrow is your lucky day," Noddy said, reading from the card. "Good! Tomorrow is my little car's birthday and I want it to be extra special."

"Ah, that is why you want the best oil," smiled Mr. Sparks, giving Noddy a plastic bottle. "Have a lovely day!"

On his way home, Noddy thought about the things he had planned for his car's birthday: he would take the day off to go on a picnic, visit Tessie Bear, eat ice-cream... "We'll do a hundred and one fun things," Noddy chuckled as he arrived at his House-For-One. He got out and put some of the special oil in his car, ready for the morning. "Goodnight, little car," he said, before going inside. Even though he was tired after a busy day driving passengers about, Noddy got all the food ready for the picnic before he went to bed for a good sleep.

When Noddy came downstairs the next morning, he did get a shock.
"Bumpy Dog! How did you get in here?" he cried. Bumpy Dog barked excitedly, but Noddy was very cross. "You bad dog, you've eaten the picnic food! Naughty dog!"
Noddy sent Bumpy Dog home and hurried out to get more food. Just as he was putting the hamper in the car, he noticed it had a puncture.
"Oh, no!" he said. "This hasn't been a lucky day so far! It will take me a while to change the tyre. Sorry, little car."

Since Noddy had set off late, he drove faster than usual to try and make up time. Mr. Plod soon stopped him.
"I'm afraid that's a speeding ticket, Noddy," he said sternly, writing in his notebook. "You know you mustn't drive that fast."
"I'm sorry, Mr. Plod," sighed Noddy, taking the ticket. He drove more carefully, but was beginning to feel fed up with his so-called lucky day. To cheer himself up, he stopped to buy some of his favourite Googleberry Surprise ice-cream.
"I'm sorry, Noddy," said Miss Pink Cat. "Someone came in earlier and bought all the Googleberry Surprise. I don't have any more."
Poor Noddy sat in his car and wondered whether it was worth trying to do anything at all.

He drove to Tessie Bear's to see if she would like to come on the picnic with him. "I don't understand it," he told his car when there was no one in. "Tessie Bear is always in."

Noddy gave up trying to have a fun day and headed for home. On his way, he saw Dinah Doll and told her about his bad luck.

"The fortune-telling machine got it completely wrong," he said sadly.

"Oh, Noddy," smiled Dinah Doll. "Sometimes bad things happen, but that doesn't mean you should forget about the good things."

"What good things?" asked Noddy.

"You have lots of friends who care about you, a lovely car, a cosy House-For-One, a pretty town to live in..."

"Thank you, Dinah Doll!" Noddy said brightly. "You're right! I have lots to be happy about!"

Noddy whistled merrily as he drove home.
"Look, car!" he chuckled, seeing a crowd outside his House-For-One. "It's a surprise party for us!"
"Happy birthday, little car," called Big-Ears.
"Come and have some Googleberry Surprise, Noddy," said Tessie Bear. "We bought all of it, so there's plenty!"
"Sorry about the ticket, Noddy," smiled Mr. Plod. "I had to make sure you got back in one piece."

Noddy was happy at last. It was a lucky day after all!

I LOVE MY PILLOW

It doesn't hurt me in a fight,
I could cuddle it all night!
It's cotton soft, with feathers inside,
Underneath is a place to hide.

Milk teeth left there will, I'm told,
Bring fairies, who change them for gold,
When I'm cold, it warms my toes,
But mostly it's where my head goes!

FOOD, COLOURFUL FOOD

If Noddy had not spotted the rainbow, Tessie Bear would have had to colour all the food in Toyland! Use your crayons or pencils to make the fruit and vegetables below look more tasty by making them the right colour.

CHOCOLATE TREATS

Noddy is celebrating Chocolate Day with a delicious chocolate tea for his friends. He has so many chocolate treats that he needs you to help him give them out! Cut out this page first, then cut out the treats and stick them on the table with paper glue to give Noddy's friends a yummy tea.
Make sure you have finished doing the puzzle on the back of the page before you start. Or, if you don't want to cut this page, ask a grown-up to photocopy it for you first.

A BIRTHDAY DREAM

Master Tubby Bear has stopped having chocolate nightmares now and is having a nice dream about what he would like for his birthday. Join the dots to see what it is, then use your crayons or pens to colour the picture.

SWEET DREAMS

I'll dream of a house made of sugar,
With fudge plants and white icing seats,
I'll dream that the path's made of toffee,
With tall trees whose fruits are all sweets,
Imagine a lemonade fountain,
A marshmallow fence with a gate,
Lollipop vines and pots full of mints,
A gingerbread bush - I can't wait!
If I think, think, think about chocolates,
Pink sherbet and strawberry creams,
If I think of fruit pastilles hard enough,
I'm sure to have lots of sweet dreams!

NODDY AND THE SNOW HOUSE

There were only a few days to go until Christmas. Everyone in Toy Town was delighted when they woke up to see there had been a heavy snowfall overnight. Master Tubby Bear went to Noddy's house and asked him if he would help to build a big snowman.

Noddy loves playing in the snow, so he was only too glad to lend a hand. He and Master Tubby Bear spent the morning making a marvellous snowman and finished it off with an old hat. "That's the best snowman I've ever seen," smiled Noddy.

"Let's make another one, so he can have a friend," suggested Master Tubby Bear, eagerly. "Oh, I'm sorry," Noddy said, "I haven't got time. Big-Ears is coming for tea later and I need to get the decorations up. You can make one."

Master Tubby Bear thought for a moment. "Noddy," he said, "I could make a special snow house for you and Big-Ears to have tea in."

"That's a very good idea indeed," chuckled Noddy. "We could decorate it, too. You make a start and I'll fetch the decorations."

Soon afterwards, Big-Ears arrived with a Christmas tree. "Hello, Big-Ears," said Noddy. "You're early." "Well, I wanted to bring you this tree to put outside your house," Big-Ears explained. "Are you building a new House-For-One?"

Noddy told his friend about Master Tubby Bear's idea. "I don't think I've ever had tea in a snow house," he chortled. "Let me help."

Big-Ears scooped up some of the soft snow. "This is perfect for making a snow house, Master Tubby Bear," he said, shaping it in his hands.

While Big-Ears and Master Tubby Bear busied themselves with the snow house, Noddy decorated the tree. "When you've finished building, I shall decorate the house as well," he told them. "We're almost there," said Big-Ears.

Once the house was finished, Noddy and Big-Ears went inside. "Well, would you believe it?" said Big-Ears. "It's rather cosy in here."

"It will be even cosier when we have tea," smiled Noddy. "Let's make a table and chairs." Master Tubby Bear came in to help.

"You could move in here, Noddy," chuckled Big-Ears, sitting on one of the snow chairs. "It is nice, isn't it?" Noddy agreed, putting cakes on the table. "Ooh, I love cakes," said Master Tubby Bear, hoping to be invited for tea.

While Noddy made some tea, Master Tubby Bear ran home. He was soon back with a vase of flowers. "I brought these from home to make the snow house extra special," he said. "They're lovely," smiled Big-Ears.

Noddy said he liked the flowers very much and decided Master Tubby Bear deserved all the cakes he wanted for working so hard that day.

Everything was ready. "Ooh, I can't wait for a nice cup of tea," said Big-Ears, rubbing his hands together as Noddy came in with the teapot.

Noddy put the full teapot on the table and told his friends to help themselves to cakes. "Building snow houses is hungry work," he smiled.

Suddenly, the teapot tipped over. "Please be careful, Master Tubby Bear," said Noddy. "It's not him," said Big-Ears. "The table's melting!"

Not only was the table melting, but the steam from the tea was making the ceiling melt, too! "It's raining!" giggled Master Tubby Bear. "Oh, dear," said Noddy, guiding his friends to the door. "We'd better get out before it falls on us!"

Noddy and his friends hurried out of the snow house and then watched sadly as it started to crumble. "Never mind, Noddy," Big-Ears said, brightly. "You rescue the teapot and make fresh tea while I fetch more cakes."

Noddy, Master Tubby Bear and Big-Ears were soon enjoying tea at last in Noddy's house. "We can make a snow house to have tea in another time," smiled Master Tubby Bear. "Yes, but next time we'll have lemonade!" chuckled Noddy.

HOT OR COLD?

Noddy soon learned his lesson about hot and cold things, didn't he? Look at Noddy now. Do you think he is hot or cold? Use your pencil to join him to the right word. Look at the other things on these pages and do the same with each one.

COLD

SNOW HOMES

If a house made of snow
Is called an igloo,
Would one for my best friend
Be Big-Ears' bigloo?

A snow house on a farm
Could be a pigloo,
And one made just for worms
Would be a wriggloo!

TOY TOWN'S SNOWMEN

Master Tubby Bear has been very busy building snow people that look like his Toy Town friends. Use a pencil to join each of Master Tubby's friends to his matching snowman.

A SNOWY STORY

Put these pictures in the right order, then tell the story about Noddy worrying that his snowman would feel cold in the night.

SNOW BUSINESS

Noddy has built a snowman and would like you to finish it. Will you keep it as a snowman or make it into a snowlady? Use your crayons or pens to add a face, hat, scarf, buttons and twiggy arms.

NODDY AND THE FALLING STAR

Noddy loved to go camping. Tessie Bear and Martha Monkey said they too would like to try sleeping in a tent, so Noddy agreed to take them one afternoon. First, he picked up Tessie Bear. "Hello, Noddy!" she called. "I'm looking forward to our trip!"

"So am I, Tessie," Noddy smiled. "This lovely weather is just right for camping." Noddy put Tessie Bear's bag in the boot and they went to pick up Martha Monkey. "Yippee! We're going camping!" she shouted, clambering into the car.

Noddy drove out of Toy Town and through the pretty Toyland countryside. He stopped at his favourite camping spot. "Oh, it's beautiful here," said Tessie Bear. "Let's put the tent up now!" exclaimed Martha, leaping out excitedly.

It took Noddy and his friends a long time to put their tent up. By the time they had put their sleeping bags inside, it was time for tea.

The three friends chattered until it was dark. "Look at all the stars!" gasped Martha. "They're like little diamonds," said Tessie Bear.

"I wish I could touch one," said Noddy, "but they're too high up." "I wish I were a bird," sighed Martha Monkey, "so I could fly all the way up to them." Suddenly, Noddy spotted something. "Look!" he cried. "A falling star!"

The star landed amongst some trees not far away. The three friends ran to see if they could find it. It was not long before Noddy saw a silvery glow lighting up the ground. "It's over there!" he said, pointing. "Let's see if it's all right."

Noddy was pleased to see that the star was not broken. He carefully picked it up. "What should we do with it?" asked Martha.

Noddy and his friends had no idea that they were being watched. "I've always wanted my own magic star," Gobbo whispered to Sly.

Before Noddy even realised that the goblins were there, Gobbo had snatched the star from him and run away with it. "Hey! You can't take that!" Noddy shouted, chasing after them. "We need to put it back in the sky, where it belongs!"

Noddy could not keep up with the goblins and gave up. "Oh, Noddy, have they still got the star?" asked Tessie Bear, catching him up.

Noddy told his friends not to worry, as he had a plan. He told Martha to fetch a torch from the tent and they made their way to the Dark Wood.

"I'm going into the goblins' house, Martha," said Noddy, "and I want you to use the torch and a funny voice to pretend you're the angry Mummy star."

Noddy ran into the goblins' house. "Help!" he cried, startling them both. "The Mummy star is cross that we have her baby! Do something!"

"Where's my baby?" Martha boomed in her deepest voice, shining her torch on Sly and Gobbo. The frightened goblins snatched up the star and put it in Noddy's hand. "Noddy stole her, not us!" they replied, pushing Noddy outside.

"Please don't be angry with me, Mrs. Star," Noddy said, trying not to laugh. "Show me with your light where you want me to put your baby."

"Come this way," bellowed Martha, moving the light beam. "Do as I say and you won't be hurt." The goblins ran back inside their house to safety.

Noddy, Martha and Tessie ran, giggling, back to where they had found the star. They wondered how they should get it back into the sky. "Let's try catapulting it," said Noddy, bending a large branch back and placing the star on it.

Martha Monkey and Tessie Bear could hardly bring themselves to watch as Noddy let go. WHOOSH! Up and up went the shimmering star, leaving a glittering trail behind it. "Let's hope it doesn't come down again," smiled Noddy.

They all watched the little star stay up in the sky. "I suppose it's bedtime now," said Martha Monkey eventually. "Yes, it is," said Noddy, "but I don't think those naughty goblins will be getting much sleep tonight...Mrs. Star!"

FALLING STARS

Noddy's falling star had five points. Look at all these falling stars and say which one is Noddy's, then say how many points the other stars have.

STAR-GAZING

One, two, three, four, five, six, seven,
I'm counting all the stars in heaven,
Eight and nine, that bright one's ten,
Oh, dear - I've just lost count again!

There are so many stars up there,
They make me want to sit and stare,
To watch them glitter, wink and shine,
I wish those twinkling stars were mine!

CATCH A FALLING STAR

Noddy, Martha Monkey and Tessie Bear saw the falling star come down in the forest. They need to find it before the goblins get to it! Use a pencil or your finger to show them which way to go.

WHAT A WINDY DAY!

Join in this story by saying what the pictures are as they appear.

One windy day, [picture] went to pick up [picture], as she wanted to catch the [picture] to the countryside. On the way to Toy Town station, it began to rain. [picture] did not want to get her hat wet, so she put up her [picture]. It was so windy that the [picture] swung this way and that. [picture] held on to it tightly to make sure that it did not blow away. Suddenly, a strong gust of wind blew both the [picture] and [picture] right out of Noddy's car! "Parp! Parp!" cried the car in alarm. [picture] followed [picture] as

she flew through the sky like a kite. "I'll try and catch you!" he called. was blown towards . She knocked his helmet right off as she swept past him! "Stop in the name of Plod!" cried , trying to blow his whistle and put on his helmet at the same time. The wind dropped for a second or two and almost landed in the pond. Hurry up, ! Another gust blew towards the and she landed right in it. was pleased. After all that, had not caught the , the had caught her!

FEEL THE FLOWERS

See their colours, pale or bright,
See their heads lift to the light,
See what different shapes they are:
A sun, a bell, a trumpet, a star.

Feel their petals, paper thin,
Feel their coolness on your chin,
Feel their leaves, some smooth, some prickly,
Some look hairy - they feel tickly!

Smell their perfumes, strong or soft,
Smell, as on the breeze they waft,
Smell them, crouch down on your knees,
Then breathe in deeply - mind the bees!

TESSIE BEAR'S FLOWER GAME

Tessie Bear has given you two of her favourite flowers so that you can play her colouring game with a friend. Find a dice and coloured pencils, then take turns to throw the dice once. On each turn, colour the part of the flower that has the same number as that shown on your dice. The first one to colour a whole flower is the winner!

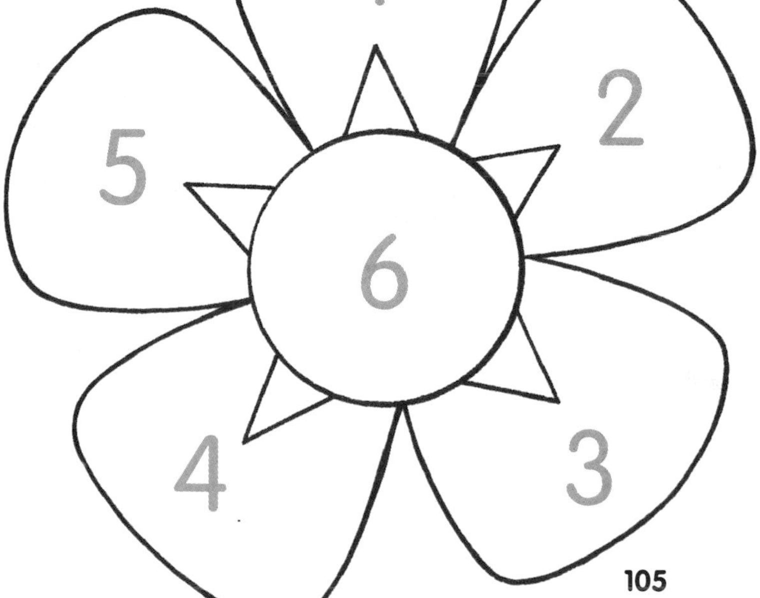

1 2 3 4 5 6

1 2 3 4 5 6

HELLO, MARTHA MONKEY

Martha Monkey enjoyed her camping trip so much that she has come on another one. She has chosen a pretty spot to put up her tent.

Use your crayons or pens to colour in this picture of Martha Monkey. See if you can match the colours to those on the opposite page.

PICK UP A PASSENGER

Noddy has just taken Dinah Doll to Toy Town station to catch the Toyland Express. Now it is time to pick up Mr. Jumbo and take him to the station, too. You and a friend can play at being taxi drivers like Noddy if you can find a dice and two counters.

START

1

FINISH

30

38

31

37

28

32

36

27

33

34

Take a counter for each player and put them on the start. Take turns to throw the dice and work your way round Toy Town to Mr. Jumbo, making sure you throw a six to start. When you reach Mr. Jumbo, you must work your way back to the station. On the way are traffic lights: if you land on a red traffic light, you must wait and miss a go, or you will be in trouble with Mr. Plod! If you land on a green traffic light, you can whizz on two spaces. The first taxi driver to get back to the station is the winner.